# THE LONELY k

## Written and illustrated
## by Truda Mordue

Sally and her brother Alan were getting ready to go to a young friend's birthday party, and Timothy, the children's pet kitten had been anxiously watching them, for he did not like being left alone, with no one for company.

Sally and Alan left the house, and Timothy followed them down the garden path. When the children reached the gate, Sally turned round and called to Timothy, "Be a good kitten, and don't wander too far away while we are at the party". Then they waved good-bye, and Timothy was alone in the garden.

"What can I do to pass the time?", thought Timothy. He sat for a minute or two by the garden pool, watching the goldfish swimming around, but Timothy was not allowed to fish in the pool, so he decided to go to the nearby woodland in search of a playmate.

3

Timothy crawled out under the gate, and scampered along until he came to a wide stream. He began to cross the water by some stepping-stones, but in mid-stream he slipped and fell with a splash into the water, which luckily was quite shallow.

A bank vole suddenly appeared, and laughed "HEE-HEE" at the kitten's struggle to get back on to the stepping-stone.

"Perhaps you would like me to give you a lift!" said the vole, with another laugh.

"Yes, please," answered Timothy, "I do wish you would help me—this stone is so slippery." But the vole was really only joking, and just ran away, still laughing, which was very naughty of him.

Timothy managed to haul himself onto the stepping-stone, and he reached the bank with no more bother. Two rabbits hopped out of a burrow just as Timothy reached the wood, and he nearly bumped into them.

"Clumsy fellow!" said one of the rabbits, "couldn't you see us coming away from our burrow?"

4

"Sorry," said the kitten, "I didn't see you coming out of the hole in the bank."

The rabbits began to move away, but Timothy called after them, "I say, don't go! I'm looking for someone to play with. May I play with *you*?"

The rabbits looked at each other, whispered something, then they ran like lightning back to their burrow. They had been told by their parents that cats were not always to be trusted.

"Ah well! Better luck next time!" said Timothy to himself, and he trotted on until he was inside the wood.

"SQUEAK! SQUEAK!" Timothy stopped and looked around him, and saw two woodmice perched on a dogrose branch.

"Hallo!" said the kitten, "You seem nice and friendly. What about a game of hide-and-seek with me?"

"What! Play hide-and-seek with a cat! Not likely!" and the woodmice scampered away.

"Oh dear," sighed Timothy, "nobody seems to want to play with me."

He went further into the wood, but had not gone very far when he heard a loud hooting above him. He looked up, and saw on a branch an owl looking down at him and calling "TOO-WHOO!"

"Hush, don't make a noise," said the owl softly, "There's a fox watching you. I would advise you to come up here where it's safer."

Timothy looked back, and saw a fox coming towards him. He scrambled up into the tree in time to escape from danger, and hopped onto the nearest branch.

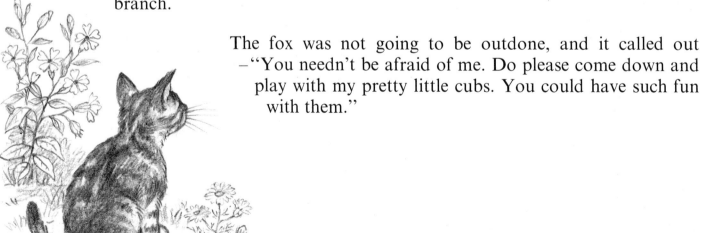

The fox was not going to be outdone, and it called out –"You needn't be afraid of me. Do please come down and play with my pretty little cubs. You could have such fun with them."

8

"Don't take any notice of that artful fox," said the owl. "It really wants you as a supper dish for its cubs!"

Timothy shivered at the idea, and hoped that the fox would go away soon. The fox *did* grow tired of waiting for the kitten, and stalked away.

Timothy jumped down to the ground as soon as it seemed safe to do so. He walked on a little way, and then stopped suddenly in his tracks. He had caught sight of the fox lying down near a rabbits' burrow!

Timothy quickly hid behind a tree trunk, and wondered what to do.

Some young rabbits came out of the burrow, and began to play, and the fox *seemed* to take no interest in them.

Suddenly, the fox jumped up and ran round in circles after its tail. The rabbits stopped playing and stared at the fox's antics. As soon as the bunnies were quite still, the artful fox made a dash at them. But they were as quick as the fox, and darted back to their burrows just in time.

Timothy was still in his hiding place behind the tree when a hedgehog passed by.

"Hi! Why don't you hide from the fox?" asked the kitten.

"Can't you see my spines?" grunted the hedgehog, "The fox wouldn't like to hold *me* in its mouth!"

"I think you are silly to believe that," said Timothy, but the hedgehog just grunted again, and went on his way.

The kitten waited until the fox had gone, and then ran off in the opposite direction.

14

The sun was setting by this time, and Timothy was giving up hopes of finding a playmate.

He wandered through the wood, until he suddenly came across the hedgehog again. It was curled up, fast asleep.

"Hallo, Mr Hedgehog!" called Timothy, "It's time you were awake!"

"Go away, you tiresome little cat," squealed the hedgehog, "I'm just having an extra half hour's sleep, and I don't want to be disturbed!" The prickly fellow rolled himself into a ball again, and was asleep at once, but soon he was woken up by a loud "TOO-WHIT, TOO-WHOO OOO!"

Timothy looked up into the tree, and there was the owl fluttering his wings for all he was worth and hooting loudly.

The hedgehog was quickly on his feet, and cried out: "That is Owl's alarm call for his friends in the wood, and it means there is an enemy around here. We must hide as quickly as we can!"

The hedgehog ran off as fast as his little legs would carry him and then vanished under a heap of dead leaves.

Once again Timothy was alone, and did not know which way to turn. Owl looked down from the tree and felt sorry for the kitten.

"TOO-WHOO-OO," the owl called out, "that bad fox is still lurking not far from here, and if you take my advice you will go back to the stream and make your way home."

"I'm going home straight away," replied Timothy. "Goodnight, Owl, and thank you very much for your help."

18

Timothy hurried back to the stream, but could not find the stepping-stones.

Instead, he saw a fallen tree trunk lying across the stream. He scrambled over the trunk, and reached the other side safely.

Timothy had just set foot on the other bank, when he heard a loud cracking noise followed by a yelp. He looked back and there was the fox half way across the tree trunk—which was starting to break. It was very old and quite rotten and the weight of the fox was too much for it. Timothy hid quickly in some tall reeds and watched spellbound. The tree trunk gave way in the middle, and the unlucky fox fell with a big SPLASH into the stream.

It was the "last straw" for the fox. It waded out of the stream and slunk back into the wood, feeling wet and miserable.

That was the last that Timothy saw of the fox, and he continued his trek towards home. He had grown tired of looking for playmates, and it was getting dark, with the full moon shining on him.

He had only gone a few yards, when he was startled by some badger cubs bounding towards him.

"What a nice little creature," said one of the cubs, stopping to look at Timothy. "Let's ask it to join us in a game! . . . Would you like to come and play with us?" asked the cubs.

Timothy looked sadly at the badger cubs, and said "To think that I've been trying for hours to find some playmates, and now when it is time for me to go home, some nice kind badgers invite me to play with them.

"Oh, what a pity," said the cubs.

"I'm sorry I can't stay with you now," said Timothy. "Perhaps I could come another time. Good night to you all."

Timothy soon reached the house, and there at the gate, Sally and Alan were calling for him. "You naughty little Timothy—where have you been?" cried the children, "We were afraid you were lost."

However they quickly forgave their little pet and led Timothy into the kitchen where they gave him a lovely supper, and afterwards played with him until bedtime.